Mallory McDonald, Baby Expert

For Becca and Adam:
you will always be my babies,
no matter how big you get.
Love, Mommy
—L.F.

For my mom, who is a great support
for my family and a wonderful grandma
—J.K.

Mallory McDonald, Baby Expert

by Laurie Friedman

illustrations by Jennifer Kalis

MINNEAPOLIS

CONTENTS

A WORD FROM MALLORY

My name is Mallory McDonald, like the restaurant, but no relation. I'm in fourth grade, and I live on a street called Wish Pond Road. There are lots of cool things about my street.

Cool thing #1: My best friends, Mary Ann and Joey, live next door to me.

Cool thing #2: Not too long ago, our new friend, Chloe Jennifer Jackson-Brown, moved into a house across the street. She's in my class at school, she's really sweet, and we do lots of fun stuff together.

Cool thing #3: There's a wish pond on my street, which means that when I want to make a wish, all I have to do is toss in a pebble.

All that stuff is great, but living

6

on Wish Pond Road is about to get even better!

If you're wondering what could be better than having lots of friends and a wish pond on your street, I'll tell you. Mary Ann's mom and Joey's dad are having a baby!

This isn't exactly news. Mary Ann's mom has been pregnant for a long time, but it hasn't seemed like a big deal . . . UNTIL NOW!

The baby is due any day, and everyone is talking about when the baby will be born and what the baby is going to look like and who will change the baby's diapers.

Of course, I don't want to do any diaper changing, but I am excited to have a new baby on Wish Pond Road. It will be kind of like when I got Cheeseburger. She was such a cuddly little kitten, and it was so much fun to take care of her.

Taking care of this baby will be fun too. In fact, I, Mallory McDonald, can already imagine how much fun my friends and I are going to have when this baby is born!

PINK OR BLUE

"Mallory, telephone!"

When I hear Mom yell my name, I scoop up my cat, Cheeseburger, and run down the hall to the kitchen.

I love getting phone calls, and I already know who's calling. It's Saturday morning, and Mary Ann and I always call each other when it's time to watch our favorite show. When I take the phone from Mom, I don't even bother saying hello. "Are you coming

over to watch *Fashion Fran*?" I say into the receiver.

But my best friend doesn't answer my question.

"We're trying to decide what color to paint the nursery," Mary Ann says.

She keeps talking before I can say a word.

"I want to paint the room pink. Joey wants to paint the room blue. Winnie thinks we should paint it bright green, which she says would look super cool, but my mom and Frank think we need to go with something softer like pale yellow."

Mary Ann pauses. "You see the problem, don't you?" I do see the problem. The problem is that we're wasting time talking about paint colors when *Fashion Fran* starts in five minutes. Still, I

don't want Mary Ann to think I don't care about the baby's nursery.

"I like pink," I say.

Mary Ann sighs. "Me too. But what about blue?"

"Blue is nice too." I look at the clock on the wall. "You'd better hurry and get over here or you're going to miss the start of the show," I say to Mary Ann.

But Mary Ann doesn't seem like she's in a hurry to do anything. "Hmm," says Mary Ann. "Picking a color is really hard."

"Why don't you paint the room orange?" I say. I try to say it in my most confident *orange-would-definitely-be-the-best-color-to-paint-the-nursery* voice. Hopefully, the sooner a color is picked, the sooner my best friend will stop talking about paint and start talking about fashion.

"I don't want the baby's room to look like a giant piece of fruit," says Mary Ann.

I try not to groan. I picture the produce section in the grocery store. "How about purple? I can't think of any purple fruits."

But Mary Ann can. "Grapes," she says. Then she makes a noise like she doesn't like purple any more than orange.

"I have an idea," I say. "Put all the colors in a hat, and whichever one you pick is the one you paint the room."

Mary Ann gasps into the phone like I just said she should rob a bank.

"Mallory, I don't think it would be right to pick something as important as the color of a new baby's room out of a hat. Do you?" Mary Ann says *"do you"* like she can't imagine how I could possibly think that would be a good idea.

"I guess not," I mumble.

Mary Ann sighs into the phone. "Be quiet for a minute while I think."

It's probably better that I don't say anything, because if I said something right now, it would be that I can't believe we're having this conversation when *Fashion Fran* starts in two minutes!

I sit quietly while Mary Ann thinks.

When she starts talking again, her voice sounds serious, like she's about to ask me an important question. "Mallory, if you had to choose between yellow and green, which would you pick?"

Eenie, meenie, miney, mo. I don't know!

Our show starts in one minute. "I think they're both cute colors. Why don't you let someone else pick while we watch *Fashion Fran?*"

Mary Ann makes a clucking noise, like she can't possibly think about TV when she has more important things, like paint colors, to think about. "You go ahead and watch," says Mary Ann. "I'll call you when we choose a color and let you know what we pick."

"OK," I say into the phone. But I'm disappointed. Mary Ann and I always watch *Fashion Fran* together. I don't have anyone to watch my favorite TV show with me. Mary Ann is busy choosing paint colors, and I can't call Chloe Jennifer because she has dance lessons on Saturday mornings.

I pick up Cheeseburger with one hand and grab a banana from the bowl on the table with the other. I carry my cat into the family room and plop down on the couch. "It's just you and me," I say to her.

I pick up the remote and turn on the TV.

I watch as the lights start sparkling and Fashion Fran's introductory music starts playing. I peel my banana and take a bite.

When Fran comes out onstage, she's wearing a silver sparkly skirt and a matching sweater.

Fran tells the audience that even though the outfit looks dressy, you can make it more casual by adding a jacket. I watch as Fran puts a jean jacket on over her sweater.

"What do you think of the jacket?" I ask Cheeseburger.

But my cat doesn't have an opinion on this topic. How could she? She's a cat. Mary Ann is the one who is supposed to have an opinion on stuff like this. But she's not here.

I put the rest of my banana down on the table. I love watching *Fashion Fran,* but I love watching it with Mary Ann. It's no fun

to look at fashion and not have anyone to talk about it with. I can't remember anything that ever prevented Mary Ann from watching *Fashion Fran* with me on a Saturday morning.

"Do you think when this baby is born Mary Ann and I will still do all the stuff we've always done together, like watch *Fashion Fran*?" I ask Cheeseburger.

I look down at my cat, but her eyes are closed. She doesn't seem to have an opinion on this topic either.

BABY TALK

There's only one thing anybody anywhere is talking about, and that one thing is a baby who isn't even born yet.

It's not that I don't like talking about babies. I do, especially Mary Ann and Joey's new little brother or sister. But how much can you say about a person you haven't even met yet? You don't know what that person looks like. You don't know what that person sounds like. You don't even know if that person likes peanut butter and marshmallow sandwiches.

So here's my question: what's the point of talking about someone if you don't know anything about them?

The answer: there is no point! But I'm the only person who feels this way.

Lately, even when people are talking about other things, somehow the conversation ends up being about this baby. If you don't believe me, keep reading and you'll see what I mean.

MONDAY

The baby talk started Monday morning at school. I was sitting with Mary Ann, Joey, and Chloe Jennifer before the bell rang. We were talking about what books we were going to read for our next book report. Mary Ann said it was hard to think about books when she's thinking about a baby. That's when the conversation stopped being about book reports and started to be about the baby, and it went something like this:

CHLOE JENNIFER: When is your mom having the baby?

MARY ANN: The baby is due any day now.

JOEY: (to Mary Ann) What day do you think the baby will come?

MARY ANN: (to Joey) I think Friday. If I were going to be born, I'd want to be born on a Friday so I'd have the weekend to look forward to.

JOEY: (shaking his head) I think the baby will come today so he gets here in time to watch the football game on TV tonight.

MARY ANN: (rolling her eyes) There's no way the baby will care about a football game.

Honestly, what I cared about was what book I was going to pick for my book report. But Mary Ann and Joey started arguing about whether the baby would like sports, and they didn't stop until the second bell rang, which meant everyone had to stop talking.

I've never been so happy to hear that second bell in my life.

TUESDAY

The baby talk continued Tuesday afternoon during math class.

We were learning how to make charts. Mr. Knight said it would be easier for us to understand the purpose of charts if we made one using data from the students in our class. He said we would make a chart that showed how many kids in the class have younger brothers and sisters and how many have older brothers and sisters.

Mary Ann raised her hand and asked Mr. Knight if she and Joey could count their new brother or sister, who would be born any day now.

When she said that, Mr. Knight actually stopped talking about making charts and started talking about babies! He said a bunch of stuff about how exciting it is that Mary Ann and Joey are going to have a new baby in their family, and then he asked if anyone else had a baby in their family.

Grace raised her hand and said that she has a sister who is two, so Mr. Knight asked

Grace to please tell the class what it's like to have a much younger sibling at home.

Grace said that for a very long time all her sister did was sleep and cry and eat and poop. Especially poop.

When she said that, a lot of kids started laughing. Usually, Mr. Knight would say something like, "Could someone please tell me what's so funny?"

But Mr. Knight smiled like he understood perfectly well why everyone was laughing.

I wish I felt the same way.

WEDNESDAY

On Wednesday, everyone was still talking about the baby.

It started at the lunch table when Mary Ann was just sitting in her seat, rolling a grape around on her lunch tray and not saying much. It was weird, because Mary

Ann always has a lot to say.

Whenever Mary Ann is quiet, I'm the one who asks her why she's being quiet. But to be honest, I was kind of glad that she was being quiet for a change.

But April must have thought it was weird too, because *she* asked Mary Ann why she was being so quiet, and Mary Ann said it was because she was busy thinking about what the new baby was going to be named.

She said that her mom and Frank like Claire for a girl and Charlie for a boy and that she likes Charlie for a boy but Amanda or Ashley for a girl.

That's when everybody at the table started talking about what names they like.

Pamela said she likes Charlie for a boy too, but she agrees with Mary Ann that

Amanda and Ashley are better names for a girl.

April said she likes the name Charlie for a boy *or* a girl.

Chloe Jennifer said she thinks the baby should get a double name like Ashley Elizabeth or Charlie Will.

Danielle said she doesn't like Charlie or Claire or Amanda or Ashley Elizabeth or Ashley or Charlie Will. She said she likes Zane for a boy and Miranda for a girl.

Arielle said she likes those names too because they sound like movie star names and who wouldn't want a movie star name?

Then everybody looked at me like they were waiting for me to say what name I liked. I shrugged and said all those names sounded good.

What I wanted to say was, "Can't we

talk about something else besides baby names?"

But I didn't.

THURSDAY

On Thursday, when I least expected it, there was more baby talk.

I was at the dentist's office, getting my teeth cleaned. I never thought anyone would be talking about the baby there. The only thing people ever talk about at the dentist's office is teeth.

But my dentist, Dr. Webber, is also Mary Ann and Joey's dentist. While he was examining my teeth, he asked Mom how Colleen was doing. And guess what he and Mom started talking about? If you guessed Colleen's baby, you guessed right!

When Dr. Webber should have been telling Mom that I have been doing an excellent job flossing—because I have been— he was talking to Mom about Colleen's baby and when it is due. He never said a word about how well I've been flossing!

And to make matters worse, he and Mom talked for a really long time about Colleen's baby, and the whole time they were talking, I was still stuck in his chair!

FRIDAY

By Friday, I thought for sure there would be nothing left for anyone to say about the baby. But I was wrong.

I went over to Chloe Jennifer's house, where Chloe Jennifer and Mary Ann and I were all supposed to be working on our take-home art projects together. But when I got there, the baby talk started all over again.

To be fair, I'm the one who started it.

I got to Chloe Jennifer's house before Mary Ann, and I decided to talk to Chloe Jennifer about how I've been feeling lately.

I told her that even though I'm excited about Mary Ann and Joey's little brother or sister being born, I don't like that it's practically the only thing anyone ever talks about anymore.

After I said that, I waited for Chloe Jennifer to say something back, like, *"I get it. Who wants to talk about the baby all the time?"* Chloe Jennifer is an only child, so I thought for sure she would understand.

I thought she would hold her nose or make a face like the whole topic was as gross as a dirty diaper.

But that's not what Chloe Jennifer did. She got this strange, daydreamy look on her face, like just thinking about a baby made her feel happy. Then she told me she has always wanted a brother or a sister. She said that she could totally understand why this new baby is the only thing anyone talks about, especially Mary Ann and Joey.

She's **NO** help at all.

When she said that, I knew Chloe Jennifer was NOT the right person for me to be talking to.

Now, it's Sunday night, and I haven't told anyone else about how I'm feeling.

Part of me gets that having a baby is a big deal and that it's something people like to talk about, especially the people who are having the baby. I just don't get why it's the *only* thing they want to talk about. And it makes me wonder what things will be like when the baby actually gets here.

I close my eyes, pretend I'm at the wish pond on my street, and make a wish.

I wish that when this baby is born, things with my friends will be just like they've always been.

I keep my eyes shut and think about my wish. I hope my friends and I keep doing the same things we've always done and talk about the same things we've always talked about. I keep my eyes squeezed shut for an extra long time. This is one wish that I really hope comes true.

IT'S A BOY!

When I woke up this morning, it seemed like today was going to be a totally normal day. I did all the things I normally do.

I got up.

I got dressed.

I fed Cheeseburger.

I ate a waffle.

I brushed my teeth.

I fought with Max about whose turn it was to clean the bathroom.

I lost the fight.

I cleaned the bathroom.

I walked to school with my friends.

I did math problems during math.

I played dodgeball in P.E.

I took a pop quiz in science.

I compared my grade on the pop quiz to Pamela's grade, and Pamela did better.

At lunch, I ate a peanut butter and marshmallow sandwich, just like I always do. I had just come back from lunch and was opening my social studies book to the chapter on the American Revolution when our principal, Mrs. Finney, came into our classroom. That's when this day went from totally normal to totally NOT!

Mrs. Finney said she needed to speak to Mr. Knight. Mr. Knight went outside with Mrs. Finney.

When he came back into the classroom,

Mr. Knight said he needed to see Mary Ann and Joey, so they went outside the classroom with Mr. Knight.

Then Mrs. Finney and Mr. Knight and Mary Ann and Joey all came back into the classroom together. And when they came back, they were all smiling.

Mr. Knight said that Joey and Mary Ann had an important announcement that they wanted to make to the class.

Mary Ann said, "Our mom just had her baby."

And Joey said, "It's a boy!"

Everyone, especially the boys, started clapping and cheering like they were on a baseball team that had just won the World Series.

Then Mrs. Finney said that Joey's dad was on his way to school to pick up Mary Ann and Joey. Frank was going to take

them to the hospital so they could meet their new brother.

After Mrs. Finney left our classroom, Mr. Knight said we could take a break from learning about the American Revolution until Joey's dad arrived.

So we spent the next fifteen minutes talking about how exciting it is that Joey and Mary Ann have a new brother. When Joey's dad showed up, he had matching *I'm a Big Brother* and *I'm a Big Sister* T-shirts for Joey and Mary Ann. They put the T-shirts on over their clothes, and then they left with Frank.

After they left, it was what everyone was talking about.

On the way home from school, Chloe Jennifer kept saying how exciting it is that Mary Ann and Joey have a new baby brother.

I pretended to be as excited as Chloe Jennifer was, but to be honest, I'm not quite sure how I feel about all this baby stuff anymore.

When I walk into the house, Mom calls me from the kitchen. "Mallory, I have some exciting news!"

I already know what she's going to say.

"Colleen had a little boy this afternoon," says Mom. "His name is Charlie."

I think about Mary Ann at the lunch table last week. When she was talking about what they were going to name the baby, I didn't really have an opinion. But for some reason, hearing Charlie's name makes me realize that this baby is really here.

Mom looks at me and puts an arm around my shoulders. "Sweet Potato, why the long face?" she asks.

I shake my head. I don't want to say anything. I don't want to sound like I'm not happy that Mary Ann and Joey have a new brother named Charlie. I know I *should* be happy for them.

Mom gives my shoulder a squeeze. "I think you'll feel better if you tell me what's on your mind."

Maybe Mom is right. I sit down at the kitchen table and start talking.

I tell Mom that I was disappointed when Mary Ann stayed home to pick a color to paint the nursery instead of watching *Fashion Fran* with me.

I tell her that I don't really like that this baby is the only thing anyone, especially Mary Ann and Joey, have been talking about lately.

I explain that I felt kind of left out when Frank brought Mary Ann and Joey matching

T-shirts and they got to leave school early today.

I tell Mom that even though I thought having a new baby around would be fun, like when I first got Cheeseburger, I'm not so sure now. "Mary Ann and Joey are my best friends," I tell Mom. "And I don't know what things are going to be like now that Charlie is here."

Mom nods like she gets it. She goes to the refrigerator and takes out the milk. She pours a glass and hands it to me. Then she puts a cookie on a plate and puts it in front of me.

She sits down at the table with me. "Mallory, a new baby is an adjustment for everyone. It's different from getting a kitten. It will take some patience on your part, but soon I think you'll see that having a new baby on Wish Pond Road will

be fun in its own way."

I take a sip of milk. "How?" I ask.

Mom nods again like the question I asked is a good one. "Well," she says slowly, "as the baby starts to grow, you will see him smile, and then do all sorts of things—like roll over and laugh and crawl and walk and start to talk. As Charlie gets older, I think you and Mary Ann and Joey will have a lot of fun teaching him all sorts of new things."

"You really think so?" I ask Mom.

Mom smiles at me. "I really think so," she says.

I pick up my cookie and take a bite. I really hope Mom is right.

BABY RULES

"I smell my favorite cake!" I say when I walk into the house. Nothing beats coming home from school to the scent of freshly baked chocolate cake.

I walk over to where the cake is sitting on the counter and start to cut myself a slice. "Not so fast!" says Mom as she walks into the kitchen. "That cake is not for us."

I frown. If the cake Mom baked isn't for us, then who's it for?

Mom must be a mind reader, because she answers my question before I can even ask it. "Colleen came home from the hospital today with baby Charlie. Later tonight, we're all going over to see the baby."

Mom starts decorating the top of the cake with cherries. "It's nice to bring a treat to someone's house when there's something to celebrate," she says.

I would have liked a piece of cake, but I guess Mom is right. It will be fun to do something nice for the Winstons—and I'm excited to finally meet Charlie.

Mom hands me an apple. It doesn't look as good as the chocolate cake, but I take a bite.

"Get started on your homework," Mom says. "When you're done, we'll go next door."

When I finish, Mom and Dad and Max
and I all walk over to the Winstons' house.

Joey and Mary Ann answer the door.
Joey is still wearing his *I'm a Big Brother*
T-shirt. Mary Ann has on her *I'm a Big Sister*
T-shirt too.

I think they've been wearing those shirts
since Frank picked them up from school
on Monday. They wore them to school on
Tuesday, and they wore them again today.
I'm pretty sure there's no rule that says
you have to keep wearing your *I'm a Big
Brother* or *I'm a Big Sister* T-shirt forever.
"Come on in!" says Frank. He leads us all
into the family room. Colleen is sitting on
the couch, holding Charlie—who is crying.

I'd like to cover my ears, but I don't.

"Sorry about the noise," says Frank.

Mom waves her hand like the noise
doesn't bother her and hands Frank the

cake that she baked. Then she walks over to Colleen and looks down at the little bundle in her arms. She looks like she has tears in her eyes. "He's precious," says Mom.

Dad puts his arm around Mom and looks down at baby Charlie. "He certainly is a handsome little fella," says Dad.

Even Max says he's really cute.

I take a long look at Charlie. His body is all wrapped up in a blanket. The only thing you can see is his face, which is as red as a tomato, probably from crying so much. His eyes are squeezed shut, and the top of his head is almost completely bald. It kind of looks like a ping-pong ball. I'm not sure *precious* and *handsome* and *cute* are words I would use to describe him.

"Mallory, what do you think?" asks Mary Ann. Everyone looks at me.

What I think is that Charlie is loud—and, to be honest, kind of funny looking. But I know that's not what I should say. Instead, I say the first thing that pops into my head. "Can I hold him?" I ask.

"NO!" Winnie, Mary Ann, and Joey say at the same time, like they're the baby police and it's their job to guard Charlie.

Colleen looks at me and smiles like she feels bad. "I'm sorry, Mallory. The doctor says that only family members can hold him the first week. He doesn't want the baby to pick up any germs."

I nod that I understand, but there are some things I don't understand.

For starters, Mary Ann and I have been best friends since the day we were born. Everyone says we're practically sisters, which means we're practically family, so I don't see why suddenly everyone's acting like we're not.

DOES SHE Look Like a GERM Giver?

I also don't get how Colleen or anyone else could think I would give germs to baby Charlie. I don't even think I have germs. I wash my hands. I brush my teeth. I go to the doctor for checkups.

And what I really don't understand is why there are so many rules when it comes to babies.

RULE #17: Older siblings get SPECIAL Shirts.

RULE #54: Families who have babies get SPECIAL treats.

RULE #311: NO one but family can touch a new BABY.

I take a deep breath and try to smile. I know Mom said that having a new baby on Wish Pond Road will be fun.

I just hope the fun starts soon.

SURPRISE #1

"There's something I forgot to tell you," Mary Ann says as we walk home together from school.

I give Mary Ann an *I-sure-hope-the-something-you-forgot-to-tell-me-is-something-good* look.

"My grandma is coming to stay with us for a week," says Mary Ann. "She's going to help take care of Charlie. It was supposed to be a surprise, but I heard Mom talking to

Frank about it this morning."

"That's a great surprise!" I say to Mary Ann. And I do think it's a great surprise. Ever since Charlie came home from the hospital, Mary Ann and Joey have been spending all their spare time with Charlie. Once Mary Ann's grandma gets here, she can take care of the baby and my friends will be able to do other things . . . like spend time with me!

"She'll be here tonight," says Mary Ann. Perfect timing, if you ask me!

"Do you want to sleep over?" I ask Mary Ann. It's Friday, which means Mary Ann can sleep at my house and we can do all the stuff we love to do, like bake cookies and paint our toenails and watch *Fashion Fran* tomorrow morning.

I snap my fingers. "I just had a great idea. Let's stop at your house and get your stuff, and we can start our sleepover now!" I say.

Mary Ann shakes her head like my idea isn't great at all.

"I can't sleep over," says Mary Ann. "We're having a family dinner when Grandma gets here."

Then Mary Ann smiles like she just thought of a great idea too. I think what she's about to say is *"Why don't you come over and eat dinner with us?"* But that's not what she says.

"Why don't you invite Chloe Jennifer to sleep over?" says Mary Ann.

I shake my head and remind Mary Ann that Chloe Jennifer can't sleep over because she has a dance class first thing in the morning. "Why don't you come over after dinner?" I say to Mary Ann.

Mary Ann shakes her head again. "My grandma is going to sleep in my room, because the room she would have slept in is Charlie's nursery now. So it's like Grandma and I are having a sleepover. I can't not be there for a sleepover in my own room."

Mary Ann makes a *you-can't-argue-with-that* face.

But I have a very good argument for that. "Wouldn't your grandma be more comfortable if she got to sleep in your bed by herself?" I ask Mary Ann.

Mary Ann shakes her head like she's thought of that too. "While she's here, I'm going to sleep on an air mattress on my floor. My mom already set it up with sheets and everything."

Before I can say another word, Mary Ann tells me one more reason why she can't have a sleepover with me. "This will be Charlie's first time meeting his grandmother. So it's kind of a big deal. You know what I mean?"

I nod, but the truth is I don't see why it's a big deal for Charlie to meet his grandmother for the first time. He's a baby. He won't even know who she is. Plus, I don't see why Mary Ann can't spend one night with me. Her grandma is going to be here for a whole week. It almost seems like Mary Ann doesn't

Who is this lady?

want to spend the night with me.

When we get to Mary Ann's house, I tell her good-bye and go to my own house.

When I get to my room, I lie down on my bed with Cheeseburger. "It's just you and me tonight," I tell my cat.

She purrs and snuggles up beside me like she likes that idea. Even though I love Cheeseburger, I want to have a sleepover with my cat *and* my best friend.

I think about what I wished for before Charlie was born. I wished that things would be just like they've always been with my friends. But I don't think that wish is coming true. I squeeze my eyes shut and pretend I'm at the wish pond. I make a new wish.

I wish my friends will realize that even though they have a new brother, we're still friends.

That means we still do things together too. I don't want them to always be doing

stuff with their new brother and not me.
"Hopefully tomorrow my friends and I
will do something fun together," I say to
Cheeseburger.

But when tomorrow, which is now today,
arrives, my friends are just as busy as they
were yesterday.

I ask Joey if he wants to meet me at the
wish pond and teach Cheeseburger some
cat tricks. I ask Mary Ann if she wants to
come over and paint our toenails.

But they both tell me they can't do
anything because a photographer is
coming to their house to take family
pictures, and they have to get ready.

I don't see why you need a photographer
to take pictures of a baby you can barely
see because he's all wrapped in a blanket.
I also don't see how taking pictures could
take all day, but that's how long it seems

to take them. It's like they went into their house after school on Friday and haven't come out since.

I don't see Mary Ann and Joey all day. Just thinking about it makes me upset. I don't even feel happy when

ARE my friends being held CAPTIVE?!?

Pamela calls me to see if I want to go with her for ice cream after dinner.

"Earth to Mallory," says Pamela when I sit down with my chocolate cone. "You haven't said a word since my mom and I picked you up. Is everything OK?"

Pamela gives me a look like maybe I have the flu or something.

The truth is, I don't feel well, but not because I have the flu.

Pamela is the smartest person I know. I decide to tell her what's wrong. She always has a solution for everything.

"Ever since Mary Ann and Joey's little brother was born, I've barely seen them." I explain to her how they're always busy doing something with the baby. Pamela puts her spoon down in her cup and looks at me like she's thinking about what I said and trying to decide what to say back.

"My aunt had a baby last year," she says. "Clarissa cried for three months straight. My cousin Henry said he thought he was going to lose his mind. He said his parents were always busy taking care of her and never had time for him. Plus, it was hard for him to deal with the baby crying all the time."

Pamela stops talking and takes a bite of her ice cream. Then she continues. "One day, Clarissa stopped crying and started smiling. After that, Henry was happy to have her around."

I look at Pamela. For someone who's so smart, I don't think she gets it. "How does that solve my problem?" I ask her.

Pamela smiles like she's happy to explain. "What I'm saying is that I think you have to be patient. I'm no expert, but it probably takes time for everyone to get used to a new baby. Mary Ann and Joey have been busy, but I'll bet things will get back to normal soon."

I take a big bite of my ice cream cone and look at my watch. It's a shame there's not a "soon" hand, because in my opinion, "soon" can't come fast enough.

SURPRISE #2

I've waited all week for Friday to get here, and there are two reasons I'm glad it has.

Reason #1: The school week is over.

Reason #2: Last weekend was NOT fun. I'm hoping this one will be better.

Last weekend, I didn't see Mary Ann and Joey at all. They were so busy with their new brother and with Mary Ann's grandma that they didn't have time to do anything fun with me. Mom said I would have to be patient. Pamela said the same thing. I've been trying to be patient, but it hasn't been easy.

I make a quick wish that my friends will be ready to do something fun this weekend. I know I am!

When I get to my house after school, I walk into the kitchen to get a snack. But when I do, I'm surprised by what I see. Mom's wearing an apron, and she's busy arranging platters of food. There are little sandwiches with frilly toothpicks stuck in them and the crusts cut off, and trays of mini cupcakes with blue icing and tiny rattles on the top.

"Mallory, I'm glad you're home! I'm having a surprise baby shower for Colleen tonight. You can help me get everything ready." Mom hands me a bowl of melon balls and asks me to put them on skewers.

She keeps talking while she fills a bowl with nuts and dried fruit. "I invited all the neighbors. Colleen thinks that just her family is coming over for dinner, but when they get here, she'll be very surprised." Mom smiles like she's proud of herself for coming up with tonight's plan.

I open my mouth to say something, but nothing comes out.

"Is something the matter?" asks Mom.

Mom knows I've been upset because I haven't seen Mary Ann and Joey much since Charlie was born. "I wanted to do something fun with my friends this weekend," I tell her.

Mom smiles. "This *will* be fun. You've never been to a baby shower before."

I give Mom a *maybe-you-think-this-will-be-fun-but-I'm-not-sure-I-agree* look.

Mom laughs. "Just give it a try," she says. She hands me a stack of light blue plates and matching napkins and asks me to put them on the dining room table.

I help Mom finish setting up, and then I go to my room to get dressed. Mom told everyone who is coming to the baby shower to wear something light blue. I start looking through my closet.

"Maybe tonight will be fun," I say to

Cheeseburger. It's true that I've never been to a baby shower. I don't even know what you do at a baby shower.

I'm about to find out.

Our neighbors arrive before Colleen, Frank, Mary Ann, Joey, Winnie, Grandpa Winston, Mary Ann's grandmother, and baby

Is this a
BABY SHOWER?

Charlie come over. Everyone has gifts, and everyone is wearing light blue. Chloe Jennifer is carrying her camera. The dining room is set up with all the food and desserts Mom made. I have to admit that everything looks pretty.

"So far, so good," I whisper to Cheeseburger. Having a baby shower with my friends just might be fun.

But the minute the Winstons walk into our house, everything goes from *might-be-fun* to *no-fun-at-all*.

Everyone at the baby shower is looking at baby Charlie and talking to Mary Ann and Joey and Winnie about how great it must be to have a new little brother.

Chloe Jennifer is busy taking pictures of Colleen and Frank with baby Charlie. She keeps telling Mary Ann and Joey and Winnie to get in the pictures.

And when Colleen sits down to open the presents that everyone brought for her, Mary Ann and Joey and Winnie start opening presents too.

One neighbors brought them all sorts

of stuff. Movies. Books. A board game. Someone bought a bead set for Mary Ann, makeup for Winnie, and a comic book for Joey. They all smile and laugh while they open their gifts.

This was supposed to be a baby shower, not an older brother and sister shower. If you ask me, it doesn't make sense for Mary Ann, Joey, and Winnie to get presents just

because their mom had a baby. But nobody asks me. Nobody is paying attention to me at all. Even though the shower is at my house, it's almost like my friends don't even know or care that I'm here.

In my head, I make a list of ten things I could be doing, and even if I did them, I still don't think anyone would know or care that I'm here.

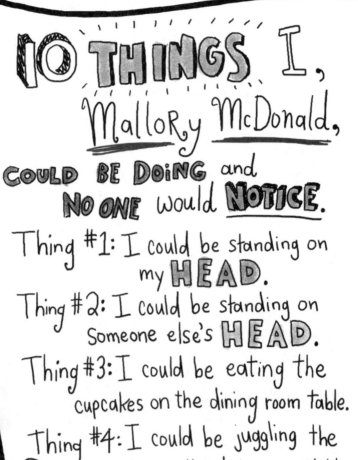

10 THINGS I, Mallory McDonald, COULD BE DOING and NO ONE would NOTICE.

Thing #1: I could be standing on my **HEAD**.

Thing #2: I could be standing on someone else's **HEAD**.

Thing #3: I could be eating the cupcakes on the dining room table.

Thing #4: I could be juggling the cupcakes on the dining room table.

Thing #5: I could be juggling the dining room table.

Thing #6:   I could be sucking on a pacifier.

Thing #7:   I could be drinking from a **BOTTLE**.

Thing #8:   I could be wearing a diaper.

Thing #9:   I could be yelling that the house is on **FiRE**.

Thing #10: I could be standing on my head, eating cupcakes, sucking on a pacifier, drinking from a bottle, wearing a diaper (and only a diaper), juggling a table, while yelling that the house is on fire, and actually pointing to that fire — and still, no one would notice that I'm here.

While everyone eats little sandwiches and miniature cupcakes and talks about how delicious they are, I try to smile like I'm enjoying them too. But I'm having a hard time enjoying anything.

When all the presents are open and all the food is eaten, everyone gets ready to leave.

"It's been a big night for little Charlie," says Colleen. "Thanks for everything," she says to Mom.

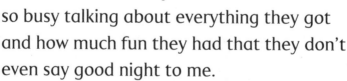

Mary Ann and Joey and Winnie gather up all the presents. They're so busy talking about everything they got and how much fun they had that they don't even say good night to me.

After everyone is gone, I go to my room.

Mom said the baby shower would be fun. It might have been be fun for some people, but I wasn't one of those people.

I lie down on my bed with Cheeseburger. "I really wanted tonight to be a fun night with my friends," I tell her.

I look at Cheeseburger. She purrs and gives me an *I-understand-exactly-how-you-feel* look. Just knowing that Cheeseburger gets it makes me feel better.

I keep talking. "I need to do something to show Mary Ann and Joey that even though Charlie is here, we can still do fun things together."

I look at Cheeseburger. It almost seems like she's nodding her head and agreeing with what I just said.

I keep going. "There have been a lot of surprises lately on Wish Pond Road. But none of them have been very good

surprises." I need to plan a surprise for
Mary Ann and Joey—and not just a good
surprise. "I need to plan a *great* surprise!" I
say to my cat.

Cheeseburger meows like she likes that
idea.

I do too. And I already know what that
great surprise will be.

I walk to my closet and open it up. I start taking out the things I need for my plan. I make a big pile in the middle of my room.

When I'm done, I stack everything neatly by my door. Now all I have to do is wait for tomorrow to get here.

Then I walk to my desk and sit down. I start writing.

First thing tomorrow morning, my friends are going to be surprised.

Very, very, very surprised!

SURPRISE #3

The minute my alarm goes off, I turn it off. I don't even hit the snooze button. It's time to put my plan into action. I was so excited just thinking about the surprise I planned for my friends, I could hardly sleep. When they find out what we're doing today, I know Mary Ann and Joey are going to be just as excited as I am.

They're going to see that doing things with me is just as much fun as doing things with their baby brother.

I hop out of bed and throw on leggings and a sweatshirt. I pull my hair into a high ponytail and quickly brush my teeth. I slide my feet into my sneakers, and I'm ready to go.

For my surprise to work, there are a LOT of things I need to do.

First, I put everything I got out last night into a big shopping bag. I tiptoe down the hall and put the bag by the front door.

To Do List

1. Fill shopping bag with supplies.
2. Find Picnic basket.
3. Fill the picnic basket with yummy food and paper plates & vase of flowers.
4. Pack up big blanket, cd player and cds and cheeseburger.
5. Set up an AMAZING picnic at the wish pond.
6. Set up the scavenger hunt.
7. Surprise my friends!!!

Then I go to the closet in the hall and carefully take the picnic basket down off the top shelf.

Next, I go into the kitchen. I fill up the picnic basket with juice, milk, cereal, bagels, butter, jelly, bananas, strawberries, and grapes. I put in paper plates, bowls, cups and napkins, and plastic spoons and knives. I even put in a little vase full of flowers.

I have to be extra quiet while I do everything. Everyone else is still sleeping, and I don't want to wake anybody up.

When I'm done, I take the picnic basket I packed and the shopping bag I filled to the wish pond.

When I get there, I put everything down and take a deep breath. Carrying all this stuff to the wish pond wasn't easy. And I still have more stuff I need to get. I wipe some sweat off my forehead.

Then I go back home and get a big blanket and my CD player. I grab a stack of CDs off my dresser. I scoop up Cheeseburger. I put the blanket under one arm and Cheeseburger under the other.

My heart is beating as fast as when Coach Kelly makes us run laps around the field in P.E.

When I get back to the wish pond, I spread my blanket out on the ground. I put a CD into the player and turn it on. Soft music fills the air.

I start taking everything out of the picnic basket and setting it up. It's a lot of work, but I want everything to look just right.

When I'm finished, I stand back and look at what I set up. Part of my surprise for my friends is a picnic breakfast at the wish pond. "Everything looks delicious and pretty," I say to Cheeseburger.

But the picnic breakfast is only part of the surprise. The other part is a scavenger hunt. Last night I wrote down clues and got out everything Mary Ann and Joey will have to hunt for. Setting up the scavenger hunt will be even harder than setting up breakfast. I take a deep breath and get started.

I make two stacks of clues: one for Mary Ann and one for Joey.

Then I start hiding the things they will have to search for around the wish pond. I hide things under rocks and behind trees and bushes. I make sure everything is well hidden.

When I'm done, my heart is racing even faster. I wipe my forehead again and look around the wish pond. Everything for my surprise breakfast and scavenger hunt is in place.

There's just one more thing I need to do.

I need to get Mary Ann and Joey and bring them to the wish pond so the fun can begin.

I tuck Cheeseburger under my arm and walk toward the Winstons' house. I know my friends' schedules as well as I know my own, and I planned my surprise so I would get them at just the right time—right after they wake up and right before they eat breakfast.

When I get to their house, I ring the doorbell and wait. But waiting isn't easy. I'm so excited about our picnic breakfast and scavenger hunt, and I know they will be too.

No one answers, so I push the doorbell again.

I tap my foot. I look at my watch. I wait for someone to answer, but no one does. Mary Ann and Joey always answer the door when I ring the bell, especially in the mornings. I can't imagine what's taking them so long.

I ring the bell a third time and a fourth time. Finally, someone opens the door, but it isn't Mary Ann or Joey. It's Winnie, and she doesn't look very happy to see me.

"What do you want?" she asks like I'm a stray cat looking for a bowl of milk. Someone needs to teach Winnie some door-answering manners.

Maybe Winnie isn't happy to see me, but I know my friends will be. "I'm here to get Mary Ann and Joey."

I lean toward Winnie. What I'm about to tell her is for her ears only. "I have a special surprise planned for them," I say quietly. I tell her about the picnic breakfast and scavenger hunt I set up.

When I'm done explaining, I wait for Winnie to say how cool that sounds and that she knows Mary Ann and Joey will love it. But that's not what Winnie says.

She rubs her eyes and shakes her head. "Do you know what time it is?" she asks.

I look at my watch. "It's seven thirty-five. I'm five minutes behind schedule, but that's not too bad. My plan was to get here by seven thirty. I didn't want Mary Ann and Joey to eat breakfast at home. Otherwise, my picnic would be spoiled."

I look down at my watch again. "Can you please tell Mary Ann and Joey that I'm here?" I say to Winnie.

Winnie shakes her head again. "They're asleep," she says. "And I was too before you rang our doorbell so many times and woke me up." She starts to close the door.

"Wait!" I say. I hadn't expected my friends to still be asleep. They never sleep late.

Winnie puts her hand on her hip. "What now?" she asks.

"When Mary Ann and Joey wake up, can you please tell them to come to the wish pond?"

Winnie nods like she'd do just about anything to get me to go away. Then she closes the door. This conversation is over.

I look at Cheeseburger and take a deep breath. "I think we're going to have to wait," I say to my cat. I pull her in closer to my side and walk back to the wish pond.

When I get there, I sit down on the blanket I spread out. I put Cheeseburger

down beside me. My picnic breakfast looks so pretty.

I pick up a bagel and spread some butter and jelly on it. I take a little bite. Cheeseburger rolls over and curls up next to my leg. I rub the soft fur between her ears.

"They'll be here soon," I tell my cat.

I can tell she's disappointed. I am too.

I could hardly wait for Mary Ann and Joey to eat the surprise picnic breakfast I made for them and go on the scavenger hunt I set up. I thought we'd be doing those things right now.

I look down the street toward Mary Ann and Joey's house. There's no sign of them anywhere. Cheeseburger arches her back and looks at me like there's something she doesn't like.

Unfortunately, that makes two of us.

A DECLARATION

This morning turned out to be an even bigger surprise than I had planned. And not a good surprise!

I push my chair back and put my feet on top of my desk. Just thinking about what happened makes me mad.

Mary Ann and Joey never came to the wish pond!

I waited for them, but they never showed up. We never ate the picnic breakfast I made.

Actually, I ate it. But I ate it alone, not with my friends. And they never did the scavenger hunt I planned for them.

I think about all the stuff I lugged outside to the wish pond. I think about all the stuff I brought home and put away. I think about how hard I worked to plan something fun and special for my friends. But all my hard work was for NOTHING!

I made a wish that my friends would realize that even though they have a new baby brother, we're still friends too.

But now I see that this wish is NOT coming true.

Mom told me I would have to be patient and that a new baby means lots of changes. She said I would see that having a new baby on Wish Pond Road would be fun.

I've been patient. But that's not what I see at all.

What I see is that my friends have forgotten about me. How can you be friends with people who've forgotten you? What do you do when you don't like the way you're being treated? I pick at a hole in one of my socks. There has to be something I can do.

I shift around in my chair to get more comfortable. When I do, I think of something.

Actually, I didn't think of it. The American colonists did.

This week when we were studying the American Revolution in social studies, Mr. Knight taught us that when the American colonists didn't like how they were being treated by Great Britain, they decided to break away. That's when they wrote the Declaration of Independence.

What they wrote looked fancy and sounded fancy too, but the meaning was simple. They didn't like how they were being treated, so they decided to take matters into their own hands.

I'm going to do what the colonists did. I'm going to write my own Declaration of Independence.

Mr. Knight told us it wasn't easy for the colonists when they declared their independence. But in the end, they were a lot happier.

I don't think it will be easy to declare my independence either. But in the end, I think I'll be happier too. At least I hope I'll be.

I don't see why I need to start from scratch when I write my Declaration of Independence. Mr. Knight gave each of us a copy of the one that the colonists wrote. If what they wrote worked for them, it should work for me too.

I open up my backpack. I take out my copy of the Declaration of Independence. I start reading it. Mr. Knight told us that what the colonists wrote sounds complicated, but it really came down to three main ideas.

Step 1: The colonists said that everyone has certain rights.

Step 2: The colonists declared their independence.

Step 3: The colonists started acting independently.

That doesn't sound so hard. I take out a notebook and a purple pen and start writing.

A DECLARATION OF INDEPENDENCE

By Mallory McDonald

In the course of friendship, sometimes it becomes necessary for one person to dissolve the bands of friendship with another person (or, in this case, two people).

Everyone has rights to Life, Liberty, and the pursuit of Happiness.

Things have been done that violate Mallory McDonald's right to the pursuit of happiness!

Here's a list of those things:

Thing #1: Mallory McDonald's best friends have forgotten about her. Even though they have known her for many, many years, they are acting like she doesn't exist.

Thing #2: Mallory McDonald's best friends have been spending LOTS of time doing LOTS of things with their baby brother, like eating family dinners and taking family photos and lots of other family things that don't include her.

Thing #3: Mallory McDonald's best friends have worn the same matching T-shirts since their baby brother was born. Not only does this violate the laws of fashion, but it is also rude to Mallory McDonald, who has always been the one to match her lifelong best friend, Mary Ann.

Thing #4: When Mallory McDonald's best friends received special gifts at the baby shower that was supposed to be for their little brother (and not for them), they were so excited about the

presents, they practically forgot that she was there.

Thing #5: When Mallory McDonald tried to be a good friend and plan something really fun and special for her best friends, they did not say thank you. In fact, they did even show up!

Because of the violation of ALL of these rights, I, Mallory McDonald, officially declare my independence from my friends.

This is the unanimous Declaration of Mallory McDonald, with Cheeseburger as her witness.

♡ Mallory ♡
McDonald

When Cheeseburger and I are done
signing my Declaration of Independence,
I put a thumbtack in it and put it on the
bulletin board beside my desk.

Now that I have officially declared my
independence from my friends, all I have to
do is act independently.

Which I plan to start doing immediately.

INDEPENDENCE

A Story by Mallory McDonald

Once upon a time there was a sweet, smart, cute, redheaded girl with freckles who declared her independence from her two best friends.

Declaring her independence wasn't hard, but acting independently was another story.

The problem was that the sweet, smart, cute, redheaded girl with freckles was used to doing just about everything with these friends—from skateboarding to sleepovers—so it was a little difficult to do things without them. But she knew it was what she needed to do.

She declared her independence on a Saturday morning. That's when she normally did fun things with her friends, like hanging out at the wish pond or skateboarding or watching TV.

But that Saturday morning, she didn't do any of those things with her friends. Instead, she helped her father sweep the garage. If you think you read that wrong, I'll write it again.

She helped her father sweep the garage.

Trust me when I tell you it wasn't what she wanted to be doing.

This is not a little girl who likes sweeping garages. But she knew her friends didn't want to do any of the fun things they normally do together.

First Steps are <u>always</u> the hardest.

Plus, she knew that to successfully declare her independence, she needed to make a fresh start, and sweeping the garage seemed like a good first step.

When she was done sweeping the garage, she called another friend on her street. She knew this friend was going shopping with her mother, and she asked if she could go with them.

The friend said that would be great, but when they went shopping, it wasn't so great for the little girl.

First, they went to the dance store so that the little girl's friend (who loves to dance) could buy some dance clothes. They spent a LOT of time in the dance store buying dance clothes. Since the little girl doesn't like to dance or shop for dance clothes, spending a lot of time in the dance store wasn't fun for her.

Then the friend's mother took them to see a movie. That sounds like it would be fun, and normally, it would be. The little girl loves to see movies. But she didn't love seeing this movie. It was a documentary. The dictionary says documentaries are films where the subject matter is presented in a factual or informative manner. The little girl says documentaries are boring. This documentary was about seals, and it was two and a half hours long. The little girl learned more about seals than she ever wanted to know.

Later that day, the little girl decided to call another friend in her class to come over and play. She thought if she did that, being independent would get easier.

But it didn't.

When the friend came over, the sweet, smart, cute, redheaded girl with freckles suggested they do lots of stuff that she and her best friends usually do together. She suggested they paint their toenails and make up hairstyles and bake cookies and skateboard.

But the friend in her class didn't want to paint toenails or make up hairstyles or bake cookies or skateboard.

She wanted to go outside and climb trees.

So that's what they did, but it wasn't really what the girl wanted to be doing.

Does it look like she's having fun?

The girl was not having much fun doing things without her two best friends, but she knew she had to keep going.

She decided it might be a good idea to do some schoolwork.

She thought that maybe doing schoolwork would help her keep her mind off her two best friends (which is what her mind was on). So she went into her room and decided to have a super schoolwork session.

She lined up her schoolbooks.

She organized her notebooks.

She sharpened her pencils.

She made a list of everything she needed to do.

Just getting ready for her study session was a lot of work. It was so much work that, once she got everything set up, the little girl decided to lie down on her bed (just for a minute). But somehow she must have fallen asleep for much longer, because when her mother woke her up, it was dark outside and it was already time for dinner.

When the little girl went to the kitchen to eat her dinner, she asked her mother if anyone had called her while she was sleeping.

Her mother told her that no one had called her.

Sadly, this told the little girl everything that she needed to know.

It told her that her best friends have a new baby brother and that they really would rather spend time with him than with her.

It told her that even though she and her best friends have always done things

together on the weekends, they wouldn't be doing things together anymore.

So the cute, sweet, smart, redheaded girl with freckles did the only thing she could do. She ate her spaghetti and meatballs, which is one of her favorite foods, but with everything that had happened to her that day, it didn't even taste that good.

Her first day of being independent hadn't gone very well.

She missed her friends. But they had not called or e-mailed or come over to her house. They had made it very clear that they did not miss her. They had a new baby brother, and they were probably having such a good time with him that they had forgotten all about her.

Her mom had said that it would be fun to watch the baby grow and that the little girl would get to teach the baby things. She tried to picture herself having fun with her best friends and their new baby brother. But all she could picture was her friends having fun with their new brother without her.

A tear rolled down her cheek. She had to go to the bathroom to get a box of tissues.

For the **SAD** days ahead.

And as the moon rose in the sky, marking the end of her first day of independence, the little girl found herself alone on her bed with her cat, her sad thoughts, and a box of tissues.

THE END

THE TRUTH

I roll over in bed and look at the clock on my nightstand.

It's only 8:15 a.m. I just woke up, and already my brain is thinking about one thing, and that one thing is that two of my best friends aren't my friends anymore. They haven't called me, and the truth is they're not going to call me. They're having too much fun with their new baby brother.

Even though it's early, I get out of bed, brush my teeth, and tie a pretty yellow bow around Cheeseburger's neck. I'm determined to make  today a better day than yesterday.

"I'm going to call Chloe Jennifer and see if she wants to come over and watch a movie with me," I say to Cheeseburger.

I throw on some leggings and a sweatshirt. I put my hair in a ponytail on top of my head, walk down the hall to the kitchen, pick up the phone, and dial Chloe Jennifer's number. Her mother answers. She says Chloe Jennifer is still sleeping.

I hang up the phone and look at Cheeseburger. "Now what?" I ask my cat.

Cheeseburger stretches and points her paw toward the room next door to mine.

It looks like she's pointing to Max's room. She purrs like she's trying to tell me something. I think I get it.

"You think I should ask Max if he wants to watch a movie?"

Cheeseburger nuzzles against my leg like that's exactly what she wants me to do.

I hardly ever ask Max to do things like watch movies with me, but now that I've declared my independence, there are a lot of things I'll be doing that I've never done before.

I scoop up Cheeseburger, walk down the hall to Max's room, and knock on the door.

"Go away!" a grumpy voice yells at me.

I ignore the voice and open the door. When I walk into Max's room, he pulls his covers up over his face. "Which part of *'Go away!'* don't you understand?" he asks.

Even though Max doesn't seem happy to see me, I ask my question anyway. "Do you want to watch a movie with me?"

Max doesn't take his head out from under his covers. "Does it look like I want to watch a movie with you?"

Max can be rude when he first wakes up, but I don't let his rudeness get me down. "I thought it would be fun to do something together."

Max pulls back his covers and sits up in bed. "That's what your friends are for."

I explain to him that Chloe Jennifer is still sleeping and that I've declared my independence from Mary Ann and Joey.

"Congratulations!" says Max. "You finally got rid of Kangaroo Boy and Bird Brain." Max shakes his head like he can't believe I didn't do this a long time ago.

I don't think Max gets it. I tell him that even though I'm the one who declared my independence, I didn't do it because I wanted to.

Max groans like I'm the one who doesn't get it. He puts his head back down on his pillow and pulls his covers over his head, so I can tell he's done talking about this.

I sigh. My brother was no help. I leave his room and go back to the kitchen.

I put food in Cheeseburger's bowl.

I pour myself a glass of orange juice, but before I can drink it, the doorbell rings.

"Mallory, can you get it?" Mom shouts from the laundry room.

I pick up Cheeseburger and go to the door. "It's probably someone selling something boring like wrapping paper," I say to my cat. But when I open the door, there's no wrapping paper salesman—just my best friends.

"Hey! Hey! Hey!" says Mary Ann.

I don't say, *"Hey! Hey! Hey!"* back. I wasn't expecting to see Mary Ann and

Joey. I'm not sure what to say.

Joey holds up a box of doughnuts. "Want to come with us to the wish pond for breakfast?"

Before I can say anything, Mary Ann links her arm through mine like she's not taking no for an answer.

When we sit down at the wish pond, Joey opens the box of doughnuts. He gives me one with sprinkles on it. He knows that's my favorite.

Mary Ann starts talking. "Mallory, we feel awful about something. Winnie forgot to tell us that you came over yesterday morning."

"We were sound asleep when you came to our house, and Winnie never even told us until late last night, right before we went to bed," says Joey.

I don't say anything right away. Just

because they brought doughnuts and apologized doesn't mean everything is OK.

After a minute, I tell my friends that I came over because I had a fun surprise planned for them. I tell them about the picnic breakfast and the scavenger hunt I planned.

"I didn't think you wanted to see me yesterday," I say.

"That's not true," Mary Ann and Joey say at the same time.

"Yesterday was just a misunderstanding," says Mary Ann.

I pick a sprinkle off my doughnut.

"Mallory, maybe it seems like ever since Charlie was born, that's all we care about. But that's not true. Charlie is cute, but he can also be tough to have around," says Joey.

"That's right," says Mary Ann. "He cries

a lot, and when he does, it's impossible to sleep. When you came over yesterday, we were asleep because we'd been up most of the night listening to Charlie scream."

Joey nods. "The idea of having a new brother is cool, but actually having him isn't always easy."

I put my doughnut down on a rock beside me. I tell Mary Ann and Joey what Pamela said about her cousin Henry and how he felt when his little sister was born. "I guess I didn't really believe that it could be so hard."

Joey and Mary Ann take turns telling me how it can be hard.

"When you watch TV, you can't hear what's being said over Charlie's crying," says Mary Ann. "Trust me. He can be very loud."

Mary Ann covers her ears like she's

demonstrating what she has to do when he cries.

I can't help but giggle.

"And our house always smells like a dirty diaper," says Joey. He holds his nose to show me what that's like.

I laugh out loud. Joey looks really funny holding his nose.

"And our house is a mess," says Mary Ann.

Joey nods like it's true. "There's baby stuff everywhere. This morning I tripped over a car seat and almost dropped the doughnuts." Joey does a demo of what he looked like.

I hold my stomach while I laugh. I start to say something, but Mary Ann and Joey keep talking.

"Charlie is our brother," says Joey.

Mary Ann picks up where Joey leaves off. "And you're our best friend. He's important to us, but you are too, in a different way."

I nod. This is finally making sense.

I look down at my doughnut. What I'm about to say isn't easy to admit. "Before Charlie was born, I thought having a new baby on Wish Pond Road would be like when I got Cheeseburger. I was really excited. I pictured all of us doing fun stuff with the baby. Then when he was born, it seemed like you were doing fun stuff with him, but not with me."

I look at Mary Ann and Joey. What I'm going to say next is important. "There's a big difference between a kitten and a baby. I guess I was jealous that you were spending so much time with Charlie. But I get it now. I'm sorry if I wasn't being a good friend."

Mary Ann and Joey look at each other like they're glad I understand.

"We're sorry if we made you feel left out," says Joey.

Mary Ann nods like she agrees. "We want to fix that," she says.

"You've barely even seen Charlie since he was born," says Joey.

"We really want you to come over and get to know him," says Mary Ann.

"When?" I ask.

"Today!" Mary Ann and Joey say at the same time.

It makes me feel good that my friends want me to get to know their little brother. Maybe it's time for me to give Charlie another chance. I stand up. "What are we waiting for?" I ask.

"You'd better get ready. Remember, Charlie is loud," says Mary Ann.

"And smelly," says Joey.

"Loud and smelly don't scare me!" I say.

I link my arms through Mary Ann's and Joey's, and we walk toward their house.

Together.

A REAL
SURPRISE

"Charlie, you have a visitor!"

Joey's words make me laugh. But they
don't make Charlie stop crying. The minute
I step into Joey and Mary Ann's house, I
cover my ears with my hands. I have to.
Otherwise, my eardrums might break.

I follow Joey and Mary Ann into the
family room. Winnie is sitting on the couch,
staring at the TV. She might be able to see

what's going on, but I know she can't hear anything.

Colleen walks into the family room. She's holding baby Charlie over her shoulder and rubbing his back. "He's been crying since you left," says Colleen to Mary Ann and Joey.

Colleen looks like she could go to sleep standing up. I've never seen anyone look as tired as she does.

Frank walks into the room and gives me a hug.

"Charlie is having a rough day," he says. "He cried most of the night, and he's still crying." Frank tells Joey and Winnie that when they were little, they used to cry too, but nothing like this.

Joey makes a face like he's glad his dad said he was a good baby, but he wishes he could say the same thing about his new brother. "So, Mallory, what do you think?" he asks.

I walk over to Colleen so I can get a close-up look at Charlie.

He's wearing a cute pair of footie pajamas. His little face is red from crying so much. His hands are squished up into tight little balls like he's upset or uncomfortable.

The last time I saw him, I thought

his crying was annoying. Now I feel bad for him. I smile at him. I wish I could do something to make him feel better.

"Can I hold him yet?" I ask.

Colleen smiles. "If you can take the crying, you can hold him."

I nod. "I can take it."

Colleen tells me to sit in a chair. Then she puts Charlie in my arms and shows me how to hold his head so it doesn't fall back. "Until he gets a little bigger, his neck is still weak," she explains.

I look down at Charlie. His nose is smaller than a gumball. His fingers look like matchsticks. His eyes are as blue as the sky on a beautiful, sunny day, and he has really long, dark eyelashes. He's actually a lot cuter than I realized before.

I pull Charlie in closer to me. "He's amazing," I say.

But then something even more amazing happens. Charlie stops crying.

"Did you hear that?" asks Joey.

"Hear what?" asks Winnie.

Joey shakes his head like he can't believe he has to explain. "Nothing! There's nothing to hear. Charlie stopped crying!"

Mary Ann gasps. "Mallory, you got Charlie to stop crying!"

She says it like she can't believe it, and she's not the only one who can't believe it.

"It's about time," says Winnie. She turns up the volume on the TV and sinks back into the couch like she's happy to be able to watch without a baby screaming in the background.

Colleen grins. "Mallory, you must have a magic touch with babies."

Frank walks over to me and pats me on the head. "Mallory, you're our hero!" he says.

Grandpa Winston laughs. "I hope she'll also be our babysitter."

Now, it's my turn to laugh. "I'm surprised I'm the one who got Charlie to stop crying."

Frank grins at me. "Trust me when I tell you it's a wonderful surprise."

Everyone nods.

I look down at Charlie. His eyes are closed now. It almost looks like he's smiling. I think he's happy, and I am too. Frank is right. There have been lots of surprises lately on Wish Pond Road—some good, some not so good. But the best one of all is right here in my arms.

JUST LIKE OLD TIMES

"Mallory, telephone!"

When I hear Mom yell my name, I scoop up Cheeseburger and run down the hall to the kitchen. I love when I get phone calls, and I already know who's calling. It's Saturday morning, and Mary Ann and I always call each other when it's time to watch our favorite show.

Well, maybe not always.

When baby Charlie was born, Mary Ann stopped doing a lot of things she always did, like watching *Fashion Fran.*

But Charlie is one month old now, and even though lots of things changed after he was born, most things have gone back to normal.

I take the phone from Mom. I don't even bother saying hello. "Are you ready for *Fashion Fran*?" I say into the receiver.

"I'll be there in five," says my best friend.

When Mary Ann comes over, we snuggle up on my couch to watch our favorite show. When Fran comes out onstage, she models matching shorts, tank tops, flip-flops, and beach hats in a range of colors.

"I like it in pink," Mary Ann and I say at the same time. We look at each other and burst out laughing. We almost always like the same things.

When *Fashion Fran* is over, Mary Ann and I paint our toenails. We both paint them light blue. We love when our toenails match.

"Do you want to bake cookies while our toes dry?" asks Mary Ann.

Usually I'd say yes, but today I have something different in mind.

Mary Ann pouts when I say I don't want to bake cookies. But her pout turns to a smile when I tell her I want to bake something else—and it's a surprise.

"You know I love surprises!" says Mary Ann.

I know she's going to love this one. Joey will too. We go to the kitchen, and I call him to see if he wants to come over and help us bake something yummy.

"What is it?" Joey asks me.

"A surprise!" That's all I tell Joey. I know he'll be over faster than Mary Ann and I can get out the ingredients we need. Joey loves surprises just as much as Mary Ann, especially ones that taste good.

When Joey gets to my house, I take out the recipe I found. When I show it to my friends, they get excited just looking at it.

"Chocolate chip cookies and brownies . . . together?" Mary Ann asks.

"With an Oreo inside?" Joey asks.

"Yep!" I nod.

"That's why they're called Surprise Brownies," I say.

"What a great surprise!" says Joey.

"Yum! Yum! Yum!" says Mary Ann.

Joey and Mary Ann and I take boxes and bottles and bags out of the cabinet. We stir and mix and pour. I put the pan in the oven and look at my watch. "We have forty-five minutes until this is ready. Who wants to skateboard while we wait?" I ask my friends.

Mary Ann and Joey both do. We get our

skateboards and go outside to the wish pond.

Joey shows us a new trick he learned. Mary Ann and I try to copy him, but neither of us can do it.

"Let's skip stones," says Joey.

Even though Joey is the best skateboarder, we're all good at skipping stones.

We look around the edge of the wish pond and find some nice, smooth stones, which are the best ones for skipping. Joey throws a stone, and it skips neatly along the surface of the water before it sinks. Mary Ann takes a turn, and then I go. We alternate skipping stones and all watch quietly as the little ripples flatten out.

Joey sits down cross-legged by the edge of the wish pond. Mary Ann and I sit down beside him. "We should make a wish," says Joey.

When I first moved to Wish Pond Road, Dad told me the legend of the wish pond. If you make a wish and throw a stone into the water, your wish is supposed to come true.

I always come to the wish pond and wish for things I want. Sometimes my wishes come true, and sometimes they don't.

I think about the wish I made after Charlie was born. I wished my friends would realize that even though they have a new baby brother, we're still friends.

For a while, I didn't think there was any way my wish would come true. But it did. And now it seems so silly. Having a new baby on Wish Pond Road is fun, and my friends are still my friends.

We do all the stuff we used to do—like watching our favorite shows, painting our toenails, baking, skateboarding, and

hanging out by the wish pond. But now cute baby Charlie is here, and we get to do fun stuff with him, too. We rock him and sing to him and play peek-a-boo with him to try to get him to smile.

It's just like old times, only better.

Mary Ann interrupts my thoughts. "What are you going to wish for?" she asks.

It's a good question. "I can't think of anything to wish for," I say.

Joey laughs. "I can! I wish the forty-five minutes are up so what we're baking is ready."

I look at my watch. I grin at Joey. "In exactly five minutes, your wish will come true."

A BABY BOOK

I wanted to surprise Mary Ann and Joey with something so that they would always remember what Charlie was like when

he was a baby. I decided to make them a baby book.

I put in lots of pictures, and I decorated it with cute stickers of bottles, rattles, and baby blocks.

Mary Ann and Joey loved it, and so did Colleen and Frank. Colleen said she liked it so much that the book is staying on their coffee table in their living room. If you ask me, that's kind of cool, because it makes me the kind of photographer whose work is displayed on living room coffee tables everywhere.

OK, maybe not everywhere, but at least on one coffee table on Wish Pond Road.

Everyone loves the pictures I put in the baby book. Mary Ann says her favorite is the one of Joey making a funny face when he was trying to get baby Charlie to stop crying. Mary Ann says that even though Charlie's face is funny looking, Joey's is even funnier.

Joey says his favorite picture is the one where Mary Ann and Winnie look like

they're about to go crazy one day when Charlie wouldn't stop crying. Joey says it looks like they really are crazy and that if Charlie ever sees this picture, he'll have good reason to be scared of his older sisters.

Frank says his favorite picture is the one of all the Chinese food takeout containers on the kitchen counter. He says he loves it because he loves Chinese food and they've

never had that much takeout. Colleen says they never will again.

And my favorite picture is the one of me holding Charlie, with Joey and Mary Ann by my side, the day that I first got Charlie to stop crying.

I like it because everybody looks happy. Frank took the picture, but he said it was a moment that didn't need to be photographed because no one could ever forget that I got Charlie to stop crying.

Frank might be right that no one needs

a photo to remember what happened, but I'm glad there is one. I'm even more glad that I did something nice that made my friends happy.

Who knows—maybe one day when he's big enough to understand, I'll tell Charlie how I, Mallory McDonald, got him to stop crying.

MALLORY'S BABY TIPS

Now that I've been spending time around Charlie, I've learned a lot about what to do and what NOT to do around babies. Some of what I've learned would put you to sleep if you read it, but the only person who should be going to sleep here is the baby!

I hope my baby tips will keep you wide awake. I also hope you'll get the chance to try them out on a baby you know. Babies can be really cute (especially when they're not crying).

Here are my best baby tips:

 **Tip #1: If it's not bothering you, don't bother it.** Grandpa Winston taught me this tip.

What he said was "Let sleeping dogs lie." I know we're talking about babies and not animals. I asked Grandpa Winston if he meant that if the baby is sleeping, you should just let him (or her) keep sleeping. He said that was exactly what he meant. He said that in other words . . . if the baby's not bothering you, don't bother him. Then he told me this advice applies not only to babies but also to older kids, animals, and most adults.

Tip #2: Make some noise. You might think you read that wrong, but you didn't. If you want to get a baby to go to sleep, all you have to do is to make some noise. I'm not talking about loud noises like banging pots and pans together or turning up your dance music to top volume. I'm talking about nice noise, like playing a lullaby or, better yet, singing one yourself. Babies love soft, soothing sounds. I promise that the more noise you make (if it's the right kind of noise), the faster your baby will be in dreamland.

Tip #3: Say "Cheese." Take lots of pictures with your baby. Babies grow and change really fast. It feels like Charlie was just born, and he's already one month old! If you take pictures of the baby with other people (like your friends or your parents or your brothers and sisters) and give them the pictures, they will be so happy that you did!

 **Tip #4: Be patient.** Babies don't grow up overnight. It takes a while—years, in fact. New babies don't do much except sleep, eat, poop, and cry. But don't worry—before you know it, your baby will be doing all kinds of other adorable things.

 **Tip #5: Don't forget to have fun.** Babies can be hard work. They keep you up when you want to sleep (at least that's what my friends tell me), and when they cry during the day, they stop you from doing things you love, like watching (actually, listening to) your favorite TV show. But just try to relax and enjoy your baby while you can,

because before you know it, your baby will be big just like you. At least, that's what Colleen and Frank keep telling Mary Ann and Joey. And if you ask me, they're probably right.

That's all I, Mallory McDonald, officially know about babies. I guess the only other thing I can say is that a new baby means a lot of change. Some of it can be hard to deal with because you don't know what to expect. But most of it is good and exciting.

If you have a new baby in your family, I hope my tips help. If you don't, maybe you know someone who does. And if that's the case, I, Mallory McDonald, officially give you permission to pass my baby tips along.

A RECIPE

If you want to do something really nice for one of your friends who has a new baby brother or sister (or for anyone at all), make Surprise Brownies for them. When Joey and Mary Ann and I made them, they LOVED them.

I promise that if your friends are anything like mine, they will LOVE them too!

Here's the recipe. Have fun making them. My friends and I did. And we had even more fun eating them!

SURPRISE BROWNIES

Ingredients:

1 box chocolate chip cookie mix
1 box brownie mix
1 bag Oreos
cooking oil
eggs

Instructions:

1. Make the cookie mix according to the directions on the box. When you have made the dough, press it into a greased 8x8-inch-square baking pan.

2. Place 4 rows of 4 Oreos on top of the cookie dough.

3. Make the brownie mix according to the directions on the box. When you have made the batter, pour it evenly on top of the layer of Oreos.

4. Bake for 40 to 45 minutes at 350 degrees. Cool, refrigerate, and then cut into squares.

5. Give them to your friends and watch their happy faces when they bite into the cookie surprise in the middle of their brownie!

Darby Creek
A division of Lerner Publishing Group, Inc.
241 First Avenue North
Minneapolis, MN 55401 USA

For reading levels and more information, look up this title at www.lernerbooks.com.

Cover background © dacascas/Shutterstock.com (clouds); © hkeita/Shutterstock.com (child's room).

Main body text set in LuMarcLL 14/20. Typeface provided by Linotype.

Library of Congress Cataloging-in-Publication Data

Friedman, Laurie B., 1964–
    Mallory McDonald, Baby Expert / by Laurie Friedman ; illustrations by Jennifer Kalis.
        pages cm. — (Mallory ; #22)
    Summary: When her best friends Mary Ann and Joey get caught up in the excitement of having a new baby brother, Mallory feels left out.
    ISBN 978-1-4677-0922-4 (trade hard cover : alk. paper)
    ISBN 978-1-4677-4631-1 (eBook)
    [1. Friendship—Fiction. 2. Babies—Fiction.] I. Kalis, Jennifer, illustrator.
II. Title. III. Title: Mallory McDonald, Baby Expert.
PZ7.F89773Maq 2014
[Fic]—dc23   20130224

Manufactured in the United States of America
1 — BP — 7/15/14

SUSTAINABLE FORESTRY INITIATIVE

Certified Chain of Custody
Promoting Sustainable Forestry
www.sfiprogram.org
SFI-01268

SFI label applies to the text stock